Magic Ballerina™

Holly and the Magic Tiara

Darcey Bussell

HarperCollins *Children's Books*

To Phoebe and Zoe, as they are the inspiration behind Magic Ballerina.

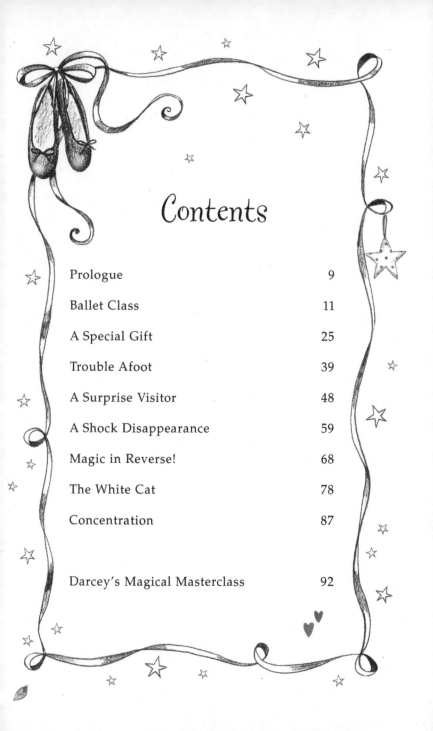

Contents

Prologue

*In the soft, pale light, the girl stood
with her head bent and her hands
held lightly in front of her.
There was a moment's silence and then
the first notes of the music began.
For as long as the girl could remember
music had seemed to tell her of
another world – a magical, exciting
world – that lay far, far away.
She always felt if she could just
close her eyes and lose herself,
then she would get there.
Maybe this time. As the music
swirled inside her, she swept
her arms above her head, rose on to
her toes and began to dance…*

Ballet Class

Slowly Holly sat upright on the sofa, her eyes never leaving the screen. She was watching the end of the ballet of *Cinderella*, her favourite bit. She caught her breath as the Spring Fairy leaped softly into a *grand jeté*, almost floating in the air, before landing gracefully. Holly leaned forward, her hands clasped tight together as she watched the dancer flutter and move with the lightest of steps. Then the credits went up.

Her mother, a professional ballerina, had been dancing the role of the Spring Fairy. *She's just the best*, thought Holly, blinking back the tears. It had been so wonderful staying with Mum over the Christmas holidays and learning the steps to this very dance herself. But now it was January, and a new school term had started, so Holly was back living with her Aunt Maria and Uncle Ted while Mum was on tour with the ballet company. She liked her aunt and uncle, but it wasn't quite the same.

Still, it wouldn't be long till half term. Holly glanced at her watch and jumped up. She'd been so absorbed in *Cinderella* that she'd completely lost track of the time. She was due at Madame Za-Za's ballet school in five minutes. She'd have to hurry if she was going to make it in time for class.

Grabbing her ballet bag and throwing on her jacket, she rushed out into the cold air.

"And-one-and-two-and-keep-in-time…" came Madame Za-Za's voice, crisp and clear, as the girls sank down in their *pliés*.

Holly felt a rush of happiness flood through her as she did what she loved most in the world.

"Push down into the floor as you straighten up… Nice work, Holly," called Madame Za-Za.

Holly's friend, Chloe, smiled at her as the class turned at the *barre* to do *pliés* on the

other side. Holly smiled right back. It was
lovely to have a new friend – up until last
term, she hadn't really made any. Her
parents had divorced over six years ago,
and there had been a lot of moving around
since. Her dad was a professional dancer as
well, and, although Holly occasionally
spent time with him, she was mainly with

her mum or her aunt and uncle.

Holly concentrated hard, as Madame Za-Za instructed the class to move to the centre.

"Use your eyes, girls! Feel the magic!" said Madame Za-Za, walking down the rows of students, tilting a head here or raising an arm there.

As Holly checked her position in the ceiling-to-floor mirror of the studio, her eyes fell on her old red ballet shoes. They might look shabby, but they were really special. When she'd first been given them, she'd never imagined

16

quite *how* special. *They looked so ordinary, but
they were a million miles from that*, thought
Holly, as she opened her arms from first to
second position.

For Holly had a special secret. Her ballet
shoes were magic! Twice already they had
whisked her away to the land of Enchantia,
where all the characters from the ballets
lived, and where Holly had the most
incredible adventures.

The class were working on a new
position now, one that the Fairy
Godmother held in the ballet of *Cinderella*.
As Holly raised her leg behind her, trying
not to wobble, pictures of the characters
she'd met in Enchantia whizzed through
her mind, finishing with the White Cat.

She couldn't help breaking into a smile at
the thought of him.

"Holly, are you daydreaming?" Madame Za-Za's sharp voice cut into Holly's imaginings. "Your hand is drooping. You've lost your extension!"

Instantly, Holly snapped back to attention. How could she have let her position slip like that? She really needed to pay more attention.

"Rise up through your spines, girls."

Holly's legs and arms were aching with the effort of holding the position, and she noticed a few girls letting go and sighing as they flopped forward.

"Lower the leg and close in fifth," instructed Madame Za-Za, then after a few seconds she added, "and relax."

There were sighs of relief from all

around the studio and someone even mumbled, "It's impossible."

But Madame Za-Za didn't take any notice. "It is important to keep the hip down," she went on, demonstrating the balance. "Not like this…"

Even in the wrong position, Madame Za-Za still looked wonderful and graceful.

"And now, girls, I shall give you a sequence of steps that the Fairy Godmother dances in *Cinderella*. Get ready to pay close attention. *Pas de chat, pas de chat, chassé, degagé…*"

Brilliant, Holly thought, pleased there would be another opportunity to hold the balance at the end of the sequence. *I'll try really hard to do it well.* She started

picturing herself with a nice straight supporting leg, but then realised Madame Za-Za was talking again. "Right, one row at a time, and we'll start with the front row…"

Holly went forward to take her position, feeling a flutter of panic in her stomach. She'd only taken in the first few steps that Madame Za-Za had set, and now she had to dance the whole sequence.

The music started and her eyes darted to the right as she tried to copy Chloe, but it was no good. She was falling behind the beat and her face was getting hotter and hotter under Madame Za-Za's intense gaze. Her row didn't even finish the exercise before Madame Za-Za clapped her hands and told them to stop.

"Holly, I won't tell you again about daydreaming in class."

For a moment, Holly felt a flash of irritation, but she fought it off. Madame Za-Za was right to tell her off. She should have been concentrating more.

As the other rows each took a turn at the steps, Madame Za-Za's corrections seemed

to ring out more and more. Then she took a deep breath and said, "Take a short break, girls. We will try again in a few moments."

Some of the students went off to the toilets and others to the changing rooms. Holly hung back a bit because she wanted to try out the steps again, but Chloe took her hand and the two girls went outside into the corridor.

"I'll catch up with you in a sec," Holly told her friend, as she bent down to rub a dirty mark off her pale pink tights.

As Chloe hurried off lightly, Holly suddenly noticed her ballet shoes. Was it her imagination or were they a brighter red than usual? They were sparkling! And now her feet had begun to tingle too. That could

only mean one thing – it was happening
again. Right here. Right in the middle of
class! She was on her way to Enchantia…

A Special Gift

A rainbow of colours began to swirl around Holly's feet and rose higher, lifting her up till she was spinning. She felt as though she was swirling through the air, until quite suddenly, she landed. The rainbow dissolved into sparkling silver and gold and she found herself inside a palace, at the edge of a grand hall.

It wasn't the Royal Palace belonging to King Tristan and Queen Isabella, that she had visited before. This one was quite different.

The hall was buzzing with activity and there seemed to be all sorts of preparations going on. Servants were rushing back and forth from the kitchen to the hall carrying china dishes, silver cutlery, lacy napkins, elegant mats and sparkling glasses.

Holly's eyes flickered to the wide archway that led through to the white and gold ballroom. The floor looked so shiny and the crystal chandeliers were glistening and twinkling. Flowers were being arranged in enormous vases fixed to the walls. What was going on?

"Oh, you're here! That's brilliant!"

Holly swung round to see her friend, the White Cat, dancing over towards her.

"Cat!" she cried in delight as they hugged each other.

"What's going on?" she asked. "Whose is this palace?"

"Questions... questions!" the White Cat laughed. "Well, first things first. The palace belongs to Cinderella and Prince Charming. And as for what is going on – well, today is the christening of their little baby, Pearl. Look, here she is now! Come and take a peep."

Holly followed the White Cat to the beautiful lacy cradle tucked in a little alcove. Baby Pearl was wide awake, her blue eyes shining as she looked at the silver rattle she was clutching.

"Her favourite toy!" said the White Cat, throwing a smile at Holly.

A small puppy suddenly hurtled by,

wagging its tail and nearly tripping up one of the servants.

"Max, you naughty thing! Get out from under everyone's feet!"

The White Cat chuckled. "Prince Charming bought the puppy for Pearl for when she's older!"

Holly was confused. Usually the shoes brought her to Enchantia if there was a problem to help sort out, yet everything here seemed picture perfect. Although, when she looked carefully, she could see that some of the servants looked a bit worried. She turned to the White Cat, raising her eyebrows. "So what is going on? What do you need me for?"

"Oh, Holly, we're all a bit fearful," he

began gravely. "You see, Cinderella can't put out of her mind the dreadful events that took place at the christening of her friend Princess Aurelia."

Holly had met Princess Aurelia – or Sleeping Beauty – before and remembered her story: the Wicked Fairy, who hadn't been invited to Princess Aurelia's christening, had come anyway, crashing in furiously and wrecking everything with a curse about a spinning wheel.

"Of course, every precaution has been taken," the White Cat went on. "I mean, obviously none of the wicked characters of Enchantia have been invited to Pearl's christening, but that is a problem in itself. You see, if the Wicked Fairy finds out that the christening is taking place and she has not been invited *again*, who knows what evil she might wreak?"

Holly nodded thoughtfully.

"Everyone has been instructed to keep the ceremony top secret, but—" the White Cat shook his head anxiously,"—you never know!" He leaned forward and spoke in a loud whisper. "Can you keep an eye out for anything suspicious?"

Then, as quickly as his brow had furrowed, it cleared and he stepped back and smiled at someone approaching. "Your Highness, this is Holly, the human owner of the magic shoes."

Holly's eyes widened as a beautiful girl with golden hair swept up on to her head stood before her. Cinderella!

"Hello, Holly!" Cinderella smiled. "I'm so pleased to welcome you here."

"I'm pleased to be here." Holly smiled. "And don't you worry, I'll be on the lookout."

"Thank you so much!" said Cinderella, before rushing off to welcome more guests.

It was so exciting, seeing the people of Enchantia at the christening. Everyone had a gift for baby Pearl, and now that they were all set out on the creamy tablecloth of the ceremony table, Holly took a closer look. There was a sparkling fan, a charm bracelet, tiny white slippers with hand-sewn sequins, a beaded purse, and many other lovely things. There was just one gift left,

wrapped in the shiniest paper of all, that
hadn't yet been opened.

Just at that moment, Cinderella arrived
at the table, looking worried. "Have you
seen my Fairy Godmother, White Cat? I
can't understand why she's disappeared all
of a sudden."

"I'm sure there'll be a perfectly ordinary
explanation, Your Highness," said the
White Cat. "Maybe she's just flown off to
get something and will be back at
any moment."

"Yes, I'm sure
that must be it,"
said Cinderella.
"And this must be
her present."

Cinderella's hand gestured towards the unopened present.

And that was when Holly noticed the White Cat's whiskers twitching. She frowned and felt her heart beating a little faster. The White Cat's whiskers only ever seemed to twitch when magic was afoot. Could something be going on?

As soon as Cinderella headed off, Holly turned to her friend.

"What is it, White Cat? I noticed your whiskers, just now."

"I have absolutely no idea why they should be twitching. It's all most confusing." Just then, some majestic music struck up and the White Cat clapped his paws happily. "Oh, my glittering tail! The

dancing has begun. My own dance is not till later on in the ceremony. I can't wait!" he added, doing a light bounce into the air, criss-crossing his feet neatly, which made Holly smile, as Cinderella came rushing back in.

"Prince Charming says I should open the Fairy Godmother's gift!" she cried excitedly.

The rest of the guests gathered round and the music faded into the background. Holly, too, rushed forward. If she had been brought here to Enchantia to help look out for spinning wheels and the like, then she must check everything to make sure she didn't fail.

Cinderella ripped off the shiny paper to

reveal a jewelled box. The princess opened it and gasps filled the air. The gift inside was nothing like a spinning wheel – far from it. On a cushion of creamy silk lay the most beautiful tiara Holly had ever seen!

Trouble Afoot

Cinderella held up the tiara. "I can't wait to thank my Fairy Godmother!" she breathed as the clustered diamonds and bright blue sapphires caught the light and glimmered and glittered like stars. "This is just the most gorgeous gift ever! When baby Pearl is older she will be able to wear it every day."

Cinderella smiled with joy at her guests. "Won't she look stunning?"

"Stunning!" came the answering cries.

"I'll just try it on myself," the happy princess went on excitedly.

Holly didn't think it was possible for anyone to look more beautiful than Cinderella in the sparkling tiara.

And, apart from baby Pearl, who had suddenly started to cry loudly, everyone was smiling and clapping their hands.

"What a picture!"

"Magnificent!"

"Where is Pearl's rattle?" asked Cinderella a bit crossly.

Holly was amongst the people who hurried over to the cradle to look for it.

"It seems to be missing, Your Highness," said one of the servants.

Cinderella raised her voice. "Missing! How can it be missing?"

And as Holly slipped back to the White Cat, she noticed the servant blushing and quite a few people staring, wide-eyed. It was a shock to hear Cinderella talking sharply.

"I guess she's just in a bit of a state because her Fairy Godmother isn't around," the White Cat whispered, stroking his whiskers thoughtfully.

That might be true, thought Holly, seeing Cinderella fling an irritated glance at the cradle, before walking off somewhere.

It was quite a relief when the music struck up again because, for one thing, it drowned out baby Pearl's cries, which were becoming louder by the minute.

"Ah, here is Prince Charming!" said the White Cat, quickly changing the subject as the Prince went over to the cradle. "He will soothe his little daughter. He always does."

But this time, even Prince Charming failed to stop the baby's loud howls and

when Cinderella stomped back into the ballroom she cried out, "Will someone do something about that baby, for goodness' sake!"

There was a stunned silence.

"Oh, my shimmering whiskers!" whispered the White Cat. "Why, oh why is Cinders acting like this?"

Holly bit her lip. She had an idea why, but it seemed stupid, so she thought she'd better not say it. Instead, she watched as Cinderella turned on the butler with a gathering frown.

"Do you expect my guests to drink out of smeary glasses like those?" she shrieked.

An uncomfortable silence fell upon the great hall and the butler clicked his fingers at the waiters to take the glasses away.

The White Cat shook his head. "I cannot believe my ears!" he said to Holly. "I could see my own reflection in any one of those

bright clean glasses. Whatever is the matter with Cinderella?"

"And what are *you* looking at?" Cinderella demanded of Prince Charming in an ugly squeal.

"Darling, I—" he tried to speak to her, but she stamped her foot.

"Enough! Why does the music keep going quiet! Turn the volume up! And dance, for goodness' sake! Anything to improve this dull party!"

The guests all tried to obey, but their hearts clearly weren't in it and their dancing was sad and flat.

No wonder, thought Holly. Who wants to dance in such an unhappy atmosphere? The fairies tried their hardest to raise everyone's

spirits, flitting and fluttering around in a series of light leaps.

But Cinderella even found fault with that. "I'm off!" she announced.

"B-but where are you going, Your Highness?" asked one of the fairies.

"To my room!" cried Cinderella, pushing over a display of lilies and leaving behind a scattering of broken china and sad bent stalks.

"Oh, my glittering tail!" the White Cat said in horror. "Without Cinderella, the ceremony cannot continue. Whatever are we going to do?"

A Surprise Visitor

As the guests milled around uncertainly and Prince Charming tried to comfort baby Pearl, Holly decided she must tell the White Cat what she was thinking, however silly it sounded.

"You know, I think it's the tiara, Cat," she said. "Cinderella started acting differently the moment she tried it on."

The White Cat's eyes widened. "You know, you could be right. She did." His next words came out quickly. "The Wicked Fairy… This must be her doing! Let's take a look at the box the tiara came in. There might be a clue in there."

They hurried over to the long table and opened the box.

"Look!" whispered Holly, pulling out a single brown feather. "What's this?"

"An owl feather!" the White Cat breathed. He gasped and his fur almost seemed to stand on end.

"What's wrong?" Holly asked him fearfully.

"Oh, my glimmering whiskers," he answered a little shakily. "I've been so busy worrying about the Wicked Fairy, that I completely forgot about any other possible villains, like Von Rotbart!"

Holly's heart missed a beat. Von Rotbart was the evil magician in the ballet *Swan Lake*. He had a hideous owl-like face and was very powerful.

"He leaves an owl feather whenever he is working his evil magic," the White Cat explained. "The tiara must have come from him."

"But why?" asked Holly.

"Let's see if we can find out just that," replied the White Cat, beginning to turn slowly, the tip of his long tail brushing the floor, leaving a perfect circle. "Let's take a look at Von Rotbart's castle," he murmured.

From out of the circle came a mist. Holly stared as the mist swirled round and round. She felt her eyes drawn in. Forming inside it was a picture of a fairy in a sparkling dress trapped in an underground dungeon,

tears rolling down her kindly face.

"I knew it!" the White Cat cried as the mist faded and the scene before them disappeared. "Von Rotbart has captured Cinderella's Fairy Godmother."

"We have to rescue her!" Holly exclaimed.

Just then, Cinderella came marching back into the room, her eyes gleaming with fury.

The White Cat took hold of the end of his long tail and swished it round again. "We must leave quickly before she notices us," he said, pulling Holly into the circle he'd made, and she saw his whiskers twitch until silver sparks flew off them. "Here we go..."

The White Cat's magic set them down in a small copse of trees.

"This is as near to Von Rotbart's castle as I dare bring us," he said, looking straight ahead. "It's possible that the evil magician will be able to use stronger magic than me whilst in his own castle, so we would be helpless against him inside. We must be very careful."

Holly followed the White Cat's gaze and saw a gigantic steel-grey castle, its dark turrets and towers poking into the clouds, iron bars at its dull windows. Then she shivered as she caught sight of Von Rotbart with his menacing owl face, appear at the doorway. It looked as though he was about to fly off somewhere.

"Look! There he is! Now's our chance. We can free the Fairy Godmother!" Holly was already rushing forward, but the White Cat put a paw on her arm.

"There could be servants or anyone inside. We need to stake out the castle… think of a safe way to get in," he shuddered. "Otherwise we might find ourselves trapped there too!"

Holly heaved an enormous sigh and as she dropped her head despondently, her eye caught sight of something twinkling inside a small shrub.

"What's that?" In a moment,

she was beside the shrub, and a second later she was waving a golden wand triumphantly in the air. "Look!"

"It's the Fairy Godmother's wand," cried the White Cat. "She must have dropped it."

"Can we use it to magic her *here* to us, instead of us going inside to her?" Holly asked eagerly.

The White Cat shook his head. "Only the Fairy Godmother can make magic with her wand," he said sadly. Then

his brow suddenly cleared. "But, of course! We could dance to make her appear, Holly! All you have to do is dance some of her steps. That is how the magic works!"

Holly looked at him in dismay. "Oh no! I knew I should have paid attention when Madame Za-Za taught us the sequence of steps."

She thought for a moment. Could she do it? She had to! There was a small silence, before a feeling of determination came over Holly. "I think I know what I could do, though…"

Turning out her supporting foot and keeping her leg quite straight, she raised the other leg behind her, making sure her knee didn't drop and lifted her arm to frame her face. Then, with a brave smile she began to count inside her head as the White Cat watched her curiously.

Holly held the position without flinching for a count of twenty, and just when she thought she'd collapse, there was a flash of golden light.

"Yessss!" cried the White Cat.

Standing before them was Cinderella's Fairy Godmother…

A Shock Disappearance

"Thank you so much," exclaimed the Fairy Godmother.

"We wondered where you were, so we came to find you!" gabbled Holly. "It's such a relief that you're free."

"For me too," said the Fairy Godmother. "But, tell me quickly, I've been so worried. Has Cinderella touched the tiara?"

Holly and the White Cat exchanged anxious glances and the Fairy Godmother's hands shot to her mouth. "She has put it on, hasn't she?"

The White Cat nodded forlornly. "She is not… herself. It's awful."

"Then we must hurry." The Fairy Godmother turned pale. "When Von Rotbart captured me, he was so proud of his evil cunning, that he couldn't resist telling me what he'd done – how he'd slipped the beautiful present in amongst the others, so that everyone would assume it was mine."

Holly and the White Cat listened as the Fairy Godmother carried on with the tale.

"Whoever touches the tiara is compelled

to wear it, and won't be able to take it off. And *that's* when the evil magic begins. It makes the wearer more and more horrible and mean, until their heart eventually turns completely to stone."

The White Cat's paws flew to his face in horror. "Oh, my glittering tail!"

"But why?" asked Holly, feeling fury mounting up inside her. "I don't understand how Von Rotbart could be so cruel. Why would he do all this?"

"Because he is jealous,"

the Fairy Godmother explained. "Jealous and angry, that Prince Charming married Cinderella and not his own daughter, Odile. Von Rotbart offered him her hand in marriage some time ago, but the Prince turned him down. Now he's even angrier at not being invited to the christening ceremony."

"So what can we do?" asked Holly fearfully. "Is there any way we can break the spell?"

"The only way it can be broken," replied the Fairy Godmother, "is if the dance of the Spring Fairy, the Summer Fairy, the Autumn Fairy and the Winter Fairy from *Cinderella* is repeated precisely. The magic of the dancing will melt the princess's

hardening heart and release her from the enchantment. Even then," she said with a catch in her voice, "it might not be strong enough to break the spell."

"What if I were to join in with the dance to strengthen its magic?" asked the White Cat, catching the Fairy Godmother's hand in his paw and looking at her earnestly. "I know the steps very well," he added.

"Yes, that would definitely help," she said. "If one of the fairies falters or gets a step wrong, then the magic won't work, so it would be good to have someone there as a backup." Her face turned grave. "Oh, and there's one more thing. The dance *must* be done before sunset."

"Oh, my shimmering whiskers!"

exclaimed the White Cat in a panic, looking up at the sky. "Then that means we've got less than half an hour to get back and organise the dance! Come on! We must go immediately!"

The Fairy Godmother waved her wand,

leaving a trail of glitter in the air, and in a flash, the three of them were whisked away to the palace.

As soon as they were set down in the grand hall, Holly could feel an uneasiness in the air. The guests were chatting and eating and drinking. A few were even dancing, but it wasn't natural. It wasn't… right. Everyone was tense, apart from one strange man who seemed to be ignoring the atmosphere and was enjoying himself, tapping his foot to the music and smiling around.

Her eyes carried on scanning the room. The Fairy Godmother had gone off to look for Cinderella, but there wasn't time to think about that now. The vital thing was to gather together the four Fairies of the Seasons and start them off in their dance.

Quickly Holly spotted the Winter Fairy and rushed straight over to ask her where the other three fairies were. The moment they were found, she hurriedly explained that it was of the utmost importance that they all did their dance right here and now.

They nodded and didn't even ask any questions which was a big relief, as through the window Holly could already see pink streaks in the sky, as the sun began to set. Her heart was thumping, when the music for the fairies filled the air. It wasn't until they started to dance that

she looked around for the White Cat. He was nowhere to be seen.

An icy fear clutched Holly's heart. Her friend would never go away when he knew he was needed. *Never.*

Something was terribly wrong.

Magic in Reverse!

The tension seemed to fade away, as everyone watched the four fairies dancing so beautifully. But Holly couldn't relax – not when the White Cat was missing, and neither Cinderella nor the Fairy Godmother were anywhere to be seen, for that matter. Where had they got to?

Turning away from the dance for a

second, she cast the most fleeting of glances around the guests – just to check. No, there was no sign of the evil owl face, thank goodness.

Holly swallowed as she suddenly realised it was all up to her now. She must join in the dance herself if anyone faltered and the fairies needed her to strengthen the magic. But would she be able to do it? Could she remember the steps?

"Concentrate, Holly!" she told herself fiercely.

She recognised the very steps that the Spring Fairy was dancing now, from her DVD of *Cinderella*. She was up to the part with the deep *chassé* then the rise on to *pointe* with the arms in fifth position.

But something was wrong. The fairy's arms were wilting. She wasn't smiling. Her eyes kept anxiously darting to one side. Then Holly spotted why. Cinderella was back in the room, her arms folded, her furious stare fixed on the dance.

Without a second thought, Holly ran out lightly and stood next to the Spring Fairy, rising up on *demi-pointe*, her arms in fifth, her head tilted. It felt so wonderful to be dancing, and from that moment on, she used all her concentration to get the rest of the steps right. She felt a lovely glow of happiness as the Spring Fairy gave her a grateful smile.

Together they wove patterns with the other three fairies until, finally, they began

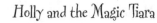

to bring the beautiful dance to a graceful
close.

It's working! Holly thought jubilantly as, out of the corner of her eye she saw Cinderella's harsh stare slowly being replaced with a look of confusion.

At that very second, there was a thunderclap and instantly a great flash of light filled the room.

The Spring Fairy faltered, but Holly concentrated as though her life depended on it, and managed to finish the last few steps of the dance. Instantly, her stomach dropped at the sight of Von Rotbart storming into the midst of the guests, his evil owl eyes glinting dangerously at Cinderella.

"You! You!" he cried.

Holly gasped as she realised the

similarity between the owl magician and the strange man she'd seen earlier. It must have been Von Rotbart in disguise!

Cinderella's hand rose once again to her head and suddenly a great wail came out of her mouth as, with a massive tug, she wrenched the tiara from her head and hurled it away.

Gasps from all of the guests, the fairies and from Holly herself, filled the room. Then everything fell into eerie slow motion as the tiara floated across the room in the fearful waiting silence, seeming to have a life of its own. A second later, it was as if the world had clicked back into place as the tiara landed squarely on the head of the evil Von Rotbart!

Everyone held their breath, and Holly most of all. Whatever was going to happen?

After a silence that seemed to go on for ever, Von Rotbart suddenly broke into a smile and walked across to baby Pearl.

"Oh my, what an adorable baby!" he said.

Holly frowned in confusion, and noticing that the Fairy Godmother was back in the room, slipped across to join her.

"I don't understand," whispered Holly. "What is going on? Why is Von Rotbart being so nice?"

Cinderella snatched Pearl up and protectively held the baby to her chest.

"So sweet-tempered," added Von Rotbart, making cooing noises as the baby broke into a smile.

The Fairy Godmother was frowning.

"It has to be a trick," Holly answered. "He must be pretending to be nice."

"And what a magnificent setting for a

christening," Von Rotbart was saying in the same kindly voice.

When he turned to gesture round at the grand hall, Holly saw his face was full of genuine pleasure and something clicked inside her mind.

"It's the tiara," she said slowly. "It's making him a nice person. Its magic must be working in the opposite way to usual!"

The Fairy Godmother nodded. "Yes, I think you could be right." She smiled, but then she frowned again as she scanned the faces around her. "But Holly," she touched her arm, "where is the White Cat?"

Holly's hands flew to her mouth. "I feel terrible. I've been so taken up with everything else, I completely forgot to tell

you, he's gone missing. I must look for him straight away."

"Wait a moment, Holly," said the Fairy Godmother. "He could be anywhere."

"Maybe Von Rotbart knows," said Holly. "I should ask him. If I'm right about the tiara making him nice, then as long as he's wearing it, there shouldn't be any danger."

The Fairy Godmother put a hand on Holly's arm. "Be careful, my dear."

Holly gulped as she started to go over, suddenly feeling a bit nervous. What if he wasn't nice? But this might be the only way to get her friend back. Taking a deep breath, she stepped towards the evil magician.

The White Cat

"Excuse me… Sir…" Holly began hesitantly. "You haven't seen the… the…" she swallowed "…White Cat, by any chance, have you?"

The owlish eyes seemed to dart from right to left before settling on Holly's face, and for a moment she thought he wasn't going to say anything, but then he smiled.

It was hard to believe that this stranger was really the evil magician. Holly waited to see what else he might say.

"I'm afraid I locked him away in a cupboard," Von Rotbart said sweetly. "I knew that my magic wouldn't work here in the castle, so it was my last-ditch attempt to spoil the dance. Silly, really, to be so mean, but luckily it all worked out fine in the end." He reached up and touched the tiara. "You know, I suddenly feel completely differently about things."

Out of the corner of her eye, Holly saw the Fairy Godmother raise her hand behind Von Rotbart's back and give a soothing smile, to calm all the worried onlookers. But Holly was getting more and more agitated by the second. She had to find out exactly where the White Cat was before anything could happen to turn Von Rotbart back into an evil magician.

"Er… which cupboard?" she asked in a bit of a stutter.

Von Rotbart leaned forward and peered right into her eyes, so Holly could clearly see her own reflection. "The cupboard under the stairs, of course."

"Thank you very…" Holly began to say, but Prince Charming was by their side in a flash.

"I have received a message that you are needed at your castle, Sir," he said to the evil magician. "May I escort you to the door? Did you have a cloak?"

"Certainly, my good chap. Many thanks." Von Rotbart was still smiling as he went out of the door, and perhaps all the way down the drive too, but Holly didn't wait to see. She just rushed to let the White Cat out of the cupboard under the stairs and to give him a big hug.

"Oh, my shimmering whiskers, am I pleased to see you!" he cried as he fell out of the cupboard. "But what about the dance?"

"It's all right, we've done it. The spell is broken!"

Then Holly went on to explain what had happened since the White Cat had been locked in the cupboard: about joining in the dance herself, the spell being broken and the tiara landing on Von Rotbart's head, finishing up on the bit about him being escorted from the palace by Prince Charming.

When she had finished, the White Cat let out a huge sigh, just as Cinderella came over to thank everyone with baby Pearl in her arms.

"I understand I was... a little... er...

bossy," she said, looking embarrassed.

"Only a little," the White Cat reassured
her. "But, of course, you weren't yourself."
Then he handed something to baby Pearl,
which made her break into a beautiful
wide smile.

"It's her silver rattle!" cried Cinderella.

"Wherever did you find it?"

"When Von Rotbart pushed me into the cupboard, that naughty puppy darted out, dropping it on the way!"

"She was crying because she'd lost it," said Cinderella, "but look at her now! She's all smiles!"

"It was definitely the magic tiara that caused her the tears too," the White Cat said.

"Well, thank goodness the spell is broken!" said Cinderella. "What would we have done without you?" she added, giving Holly another very grateful smile.

Then she turned to the guests. "The danger is past! Let the christening ceremony continue!"

Holly loved it when the Fairy Godmother bestowed the gift of a long and happy life upon baby Pearl, and everyone broke into applause. And she loved the dancing even more, especially the White Cat's leaping and turning solo.

"Help yourselves to the delicious food!" came Prince Charming's cheerful voice.

"Try one of these fairy cakes!" urged the White Cat. "I can highly recommend them, you know."

85

But hardly a morsel had passed Holly's lips before she felt a tingling in her toes.

"It's time for me to go back to the real world, Cat," she said, hugging him. "I'll see you again soon!"

The White Cat gave her a little wave as Holly found herself surrounded by the brightest of colours swirling, before whirling her away.

Concentration

Holly stretched up from rubbing at the dirty mark on her tights. It was incredible the way that she always got back from Enchantia to find that not a single second of time had passed in the real world. She hurried after Chloe, feeling a lovely glow inside her at the memory of all that had just happened.

"Right, let us try another *enchainement*, to use the proper balletic word for a sequence of steps," said Madame Za-Za, a few minutes later.

The class stood in neat rows just as before, but this time when her teacher went through the steps, Holly concentrated with all her might. *I'll always make sure I do that from now on*, she told herself firmly, thinking back to her dance with the Spring Fairy and imagining how awful it would have been if she'd not been able to join in.

"Well done!" said Madame Za-Za, breaking into a smile after Holly's row had performed the steps. "When you concentrate, you dance like a dream!"

Her praise seemed to be for all the girls,

but her gaze was on Holly. "*Always*
remember how important concentrating is."

And as their eyes met, Holly felt she
really understood.

Yes I will, I really will, she thought from
the bottom of her heart.

Darcey's Magical Masterclass

*Prepare to be crowned with the
magic tiara by doing this simple,
elegant breathing exercise.*

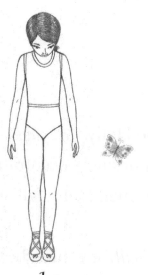

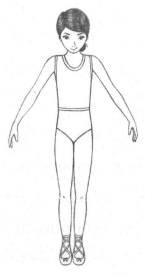

1.
Stand with your feet together,
arms relaxed at your sides and
your head bowed forward so
your chin is touching your chest.

2.
Start to breathe in, raising your
head and lifting your arms out
sideways. Keep breathing in!

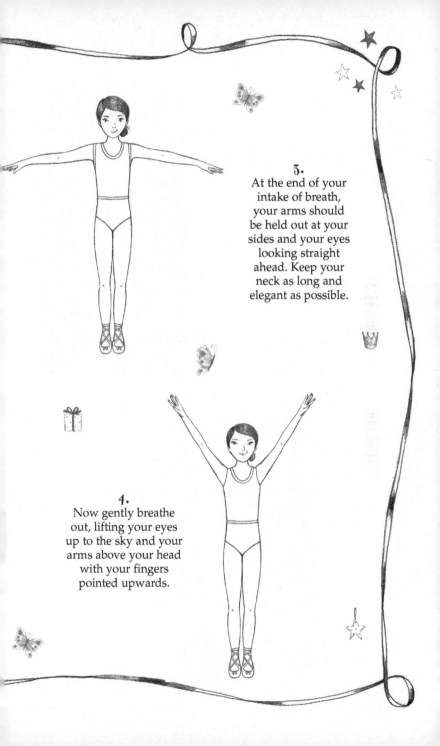

3.
At the end of your intake of breath, your arms should be held out at your sides and your eyes looking straight ahead. Keep your neck as long and elegant as possible.

4.
Now gently breathe out, lifting your eyes up to the sky and your arms above your head with your fingers pointed upwards.

Magic Ballerina

Holly and the Rose Garden

When Holly finds herself in a magical
rose garden, she realises that the story of
Beauty and the Beast is being played out,
in front of her very eyes!

Read on for a sneak preview
of Holly's next adventure...

°◎˙⁎˙☆˙◎˙⁎˙☆˙◎˙⁎˙☆˙◎˙⁎˙°

Holly's feet touched down on solid ground and as the magical haze cleared, she saw that she was standing in a beautiful garden. There were roses everywhere – white ones, red ones, pink ones. Holly looked about her. Where was she? And where was her friend the White Cat? He was usually there to meet her whenever she arrived in Enchantia.

But just at that moment, Holly heard a loud shrieking cry.

"H… hello?" Holly called warily.

There was another loud shriek and out from behind a white bush strode a peacock. His body was a bright blue and he had golden eyes. On his head was a crest that looked almost like a little crown. His long tail of feathers trailed on the ground after him. Seeing Holly, he stared.

Holly stepped backwards uncertainly. The bird's beak looked very sharp and he had sharp claws on his feet too.

He looked her up and down intently and then his eyes seemed suddenly to glitter with approval. "Well, hellllllo there!" His tail feathers rose and snapped open, like an enormous fan. "And who might you be, my pretty little one?"

"I'm Holly," she stammered.

The peacock stalked towards her. "Do you come here often?"

"Um…" Holly said. "Well…"

"No tail, but what fabulous feathers you have," the peacock interrupted, examining her feathery headdress. "I like them!"

°ⓖ˙⋆˙☆˙ⓖ˙⋆˙☆˙ⓖ˙⋆˙☆˙ⓖ˙⋆˙°

Magic Ballerina™

Read all of Holly's adventures!